HALLOWEEN PARTY

Steve Barlow and Steve Skidmore

Illustrated by Alex Lopez

Franklin Watts
First published in Great Britain in 2016 by The Watts Publishing Group

Credits
Series Editor: Adrian Cole
Design Manager: Peter Scoulding
Cover Designer: Cathryn Gilbert
Illustrations: Alex Lopez

HB ISBN 978 1 4451 4387 3
PB ISBN 978 1 4451 4389 7
Library ebook ISBN 978 1 4451 4388 0

Printed in China.

MIX
Paper from
responsible sources
FSC® C104740
FSC
www.fsc.org

Franklin Watts
An imprint of
Hachette Children's Group
Part of The Watts Publishing Group
Carmelite House
50 Victoria Embankment
London EC4Y 0DZ

An Hachette UK Company
www.hachette.co.uk

www.franklinwatts.co.uk

Lin.

Danny.

Sam.

"I'm going as a vampire,"
said Britney. "What are you going as, Lin?
A witch?"
Lin said nothing.

"We will win those prizes!" said Clogger Mills. "Our scary costumes will be the best!"

"We can't let Clogger win," said Danny.

"But I haven't got a costume."

"I haven't got one either," moaned Sam.

"What about the store room?" said Lin.

"That has lots of costumes."

"I'd hide from you," said Lin.

Danny shook his head. "No. There will
be loads of vampires at the party."

"What's your idea then?" asked Sam.

"Over my dead body!" snarled Lin.

"I hate that story!"

"Okay, okay," said Danny. "What's
your idea then, Lin?"

"Now that is scary. You'd look
weird in a dress, Lin," said Sam.
"Yeah," agreed Danny. "Plus,
it has sparkles."
Lin shook her head.

Lin sighed. "There are no scary costumes here."

"Hey!" said Sam. "I've got an idea! Why don't we go as ourselves?"

26

Mr Broad gave out the prizes.

"And the prizes go to... Sam,

Lin and Danny!"